A Read-Together Book for Parents & Children™

Sometimes a Family Has to Move

by Jane Werner Watson

Robert E. Switzer, M.D.
Former Director of the Children's Division
The Menninger Clinic

J. Cotter Hirschberg, M.D.
William C. Menninger Distinguished Professor
of Psychiatry, The Menninger Clinic

with pictures by Irene Trivas

Crown Publishers, Inc., New York

Text copyright © 1988 by Jane Werner Watson, J. Cotter Hirschberg, Robert E. Switzer.
Illustrations copyright © 1988 by Irene Trivas
Published by Crown Publishers, Inc., 225 Park Avenue South, New York, New York
10003 and represented in Canada by the Canadian MANDA Group
CROWN is a trademark of Crown Publishers, Inc.
Manufactured in Hong Kong

Library of Congress Cataloging-in-Publication Data
Watson, Jane Werner, 1915–
    Sometimes a family has to move.
    Summary: Mom and Dad help to allay a young child's fears about moving to a new
house.
    [1. Moving, Household—Fiction]   I. Trivas, Irene, ill.   II. Title.
PZ7.W3274So 1987   [E]   87-473
ISBN 0-517-56593-5

10 9 8 7 6 5 4 3 2 1

First Edition

NOTE TO PARENTS

Years ago most people were born, grew up, and grew old in the same town, often in the very same house. That is seldom true anymore in our mobile society. In any one year one family in every four moves at least across a county line. Some schools have more children transferring in and out during the school year than their total enrollment at any one time.

These moves bring times of stress for everyone in the family. Because the parents themselves often feel so much concern and sense of loss, it may be difficult for them to discuss the situation with a child. They may feel that they can spare the child discomfort by not mentioning the change ahead of time. This is an error. It is only with understanding and help from the parents that the move can be made into a growth experience rather than an emotional shock.

When it is known that a move is forthcoming, the plan should be discussed with the child. Admittedly this is often not easy for the parents, because of their own mixed feelings. This book, putting the attendant problems in the form of a simple story, is planned to help parents in approaching the subject and the young child in mastering anxiety about the move and seeing it as one of the events in growing up.

It will be of great help to the child to know about the move well in advance, to hear about the new home and community, and become familiar with the idea of the change while still in the security of the old home. The youngster should be told the reason for the move, so that it will seem reasonable and necessary, and should have an opportunity to talk out the probable fears and feelings of loss.

Important points to stress are that the family will still be together after the move, that special toys and familiar household goods will go along, and that old friends and places will not be forgotten. The child should also be allowed to know that parents and other children have mixed feelings about the move too. Leaving familiar places and people and changing familiar routines will be a major adjustment for everyone.

It is often helpful to turn some of these concerns into play patterns—packing toys for the move, playing at being a moving man, and so on. But most children will have anxieties they cannot entirely resolve through play. They will ask questions over and over again. They may become irritable, have disturbances in their sleep, and go back to behavior patterns of younger years. Since parents have their own anxieties to deal with at the same time, it is not always easy to be patient and supportive, but it is important to make the effort. Every member of the family needs to give support to the others throughout the whole move, and to receive support in return. This sharing can help the child—and the parents—to bridge the transition from old to new happily.

ROBERT E. SWITZER, M.D.
Former Director of the Children's Division
The Menninger Clinic

J. COTTER HIRSCHBERG, M.D.
William C. Menninger Distinguished Professor of Psychiatry
The Menninger Clinic

One day Daddy came home
with big news for us all.
He was going to work
in a new town.
"And leave us?" I asked.
Daddy laughed.
"How could I get along
without you?" he asked.
"We are all moving.
We will have a new home.
Won't that be fun?"

I wasn't sure.
I liked our home.
I had lived in it
as long as I could remember.

I knew it all so well.
I knew my room and my bed
and the place for my things.

I knew my play places
and the neighbors,
and our friends in the stores
where I went with Mother.
I knew my preschool.
I didn't know anything
about this new home.
I didn't even know
what it looked like.
I wasn't sure I wanted to go.

Mommy and Daddy sounded
happy and excited, though,
when they talked about it.
So I thought maybe
it would be all right.

One good thing was
that it wasn't going to happen right away.
We had time to get ready.
Daddy told us about the new town.
It sounded nice.

He brought me a toy moving van.
I played moving man with my toys.
I took my moving van
to school for show and tell.

Daddy brought me a map too.
It showed the roads
from our old town
to our new town.
He circled our old home
and our new home on the map,
so I could show it to people.

I asked Mommy and Daddy
lots of questions
about moving.
Sometimes it made me feel scared.
I thought of all the friends
and playmates I would lose.
I couldn't imagine
what new friends would be like,
or our new home, or anything.

I didn't want to go,
but there wasn't anything
I could do about it.
I felt small and helpless.
I felt like a baby,
and sometimes I acted like one.
I got fussy and cross.
Some nights I didn't sleep well.
I cried and said
I didn't want to move.

Sometimes I felt angry
about Daddy's new job.
I wanted Daddy and Mommy
to feel as lost as I did.
Sometimes I even acted mean.
Mommy and Daddy understood.

They said they didn't like
leaving their friends
and our home
and everything they knew so well.
But they said we would find
that our new home
and the new town
and new friends were just as nice.

They said the move
was a good thing.
And we would all be together.
That was the best thing
about the move.
We talked about it a lot.
Mommy and Daddy played
moving games with me.

I told all my toy animals
about the move
so they would understand
and not be afraid.
And I practiced packing
my own special suitcase.

Moving day was getting
closer and closer.
Then it began to be exciting.
The preschool had a party
to say good-bye.
Mommy and Daddy's friends
had a party for them.

I told my barber and my doctor
and the mailman and the people where we shop
and lots of other people
that we were moving.
They said they would miss me,
but they also said the new place sounded great.
I knew I would have
a new doctor and barber.
I will meet lots of new friends.

I will remember the old ones, too.
I will miss them sometimes.
But I was getting anxious now
to meet the new ones.
Daddy took pictures of my friends
and wrote down their addresses
so we could write and send pictures
after we got to our new home.

Then moving day came.
Mommy was awfully busy.
I was busy too.
I watched the men pack the van.

I wanted to be sure
that everything important got on it.
I showed the driver my map
so he would know how to get
to our new home.

After we got the van filled
we promised to meet the driver
at the new house.
When we left the old house,
we were sad and happy
at the same time.
On the way to the new house
we talked about our old home
and our old friends.

But we talked more
about the new town
and what fun we would have
all together in our new home.
We followed the roads on my map
and we found the new house.
The moving van found it too.

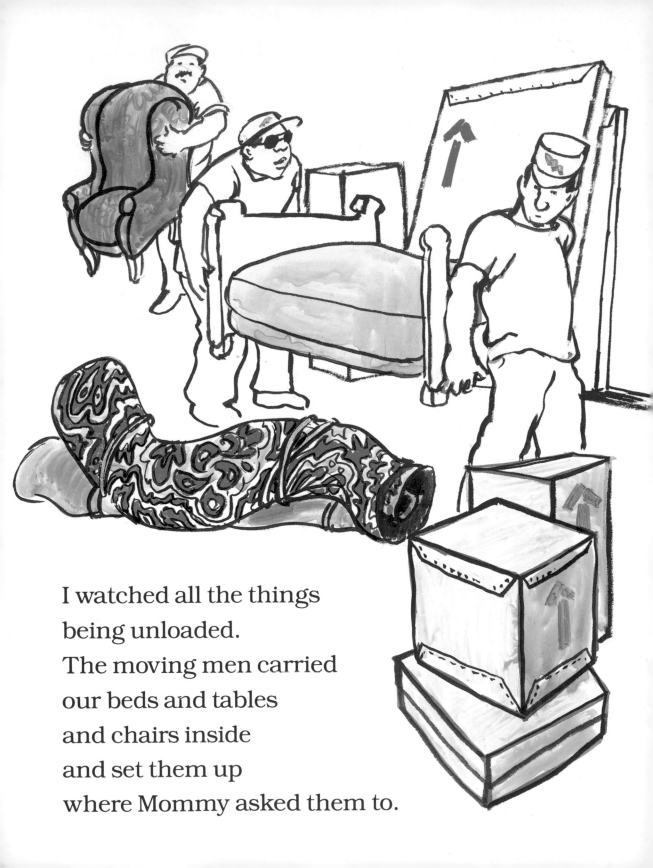

I watched all the things
being unloaded.
The moving men carried
our beds and tables
and chairs inside
and set them up
where Mommy asked them to.

Soon I could see my old bed
and other things
from my old room.
I was glad to see
those things I knew
from our old home.

But it seemed strange
going to sleep in the new room.
I was glad I had my favorite toy.
When I woke up in the morning,
I could not think where I was.
Then I remembered.
I was in our new house!

At first we were all very busy.
We had so much to do
and so many new people to meet.
There were new children
and new places to play.
But sometimes I wished
we were back in our old home.

I missed my old friends.
I even dreamed about them.
I felt sad, and then I felt
as if I were little again,
back when I didn't know
how to do things so well.
I even wet my bed a few times.

I didn't like sleeping
in the new room.
I wanted to be sure
Mommy and Daddy were nearby
all the time.
If I could hear them at night,
I felt better.
I liked to be close to them,
and we talked a lot
about how we felt.
Talking about it
made me feel better.

I started in a new preschool
and I began to make new friends.
We sent picture postcards
to some of our old friends.
We even talked to some of them
on the phone.

But now it was more fun
to play with the new children.
Mommy and Daddy
made new friends too.
I have as many friends
in our new neighborhood now
as I had in our old town.
I still remember
the old home and old friends.

But I like our new house.
I like my new friends.
I like my doctor and my barber
and the mailman and the people where we shop
and lots of other people.
This is my home now
and I like it fine.